THIS CANDLEWICK BOOK BELONGS TO:

_____

_____

_____

_____

Crow's
farm

Cow's
farm

Sparrow's
farm

Drake's
farm

Pig's
farm

Sheep's
farm

Minnow's
farm

To my dad, with love
— M. S.

Illustrations and Illustrator Notes copyright © 1999 by Melissa Sweet
Foreword copyright © 1999 by John Langstaff

First paperback edition 2001

The Library of Congress has cataloged the hardcover edition as follows:

On Christmas Day in the morning: a traditional carol / illustrated by
Melissa Sweet ; foreword by John Langstaff. — 1st ed.
p.   cm.
Summary: Illustrated verses for this traditional English folk song
present different animals tending to their crops and harvesting
them for a Christmas feast.
ISBN 0-7636-0375-9 (hardcover)
1. Folk songs, English — England — Texts. [1. Christmas music — Texts.
2. Folk songs — England. 3. Christmas music. 4. Animals — Songs and
music.] I. Sweet, Melissa, ill. II. Langstaff, John M. III. There was a
pig went out to dig.
PZ8.3.C4586   1999
782.42'12723'0268 — dc21   98-51122
ISBN 0-7636-1055-0 (paperback)

2 4 6 8 10 9 7 5 3 1

Printed in Hong Kong

This book was typeset in Narcissus Solid.
The illustrations were done in watercolor, gouache, and collage.
Hand-lettered title and music by Jenna LaReau.

Candlewick Press
2067 Massachusetts Avenue
Cambridge, Massachusetts 02140

visit us at www.candlewick.com

A TRADITIONAL CAROL

On Christmas Day in the Morning

ILLUSTRATED BY

Melissa Sweet

CANDLEWICK PRESS
CAMBRIDGE, MASSACHUSETTS

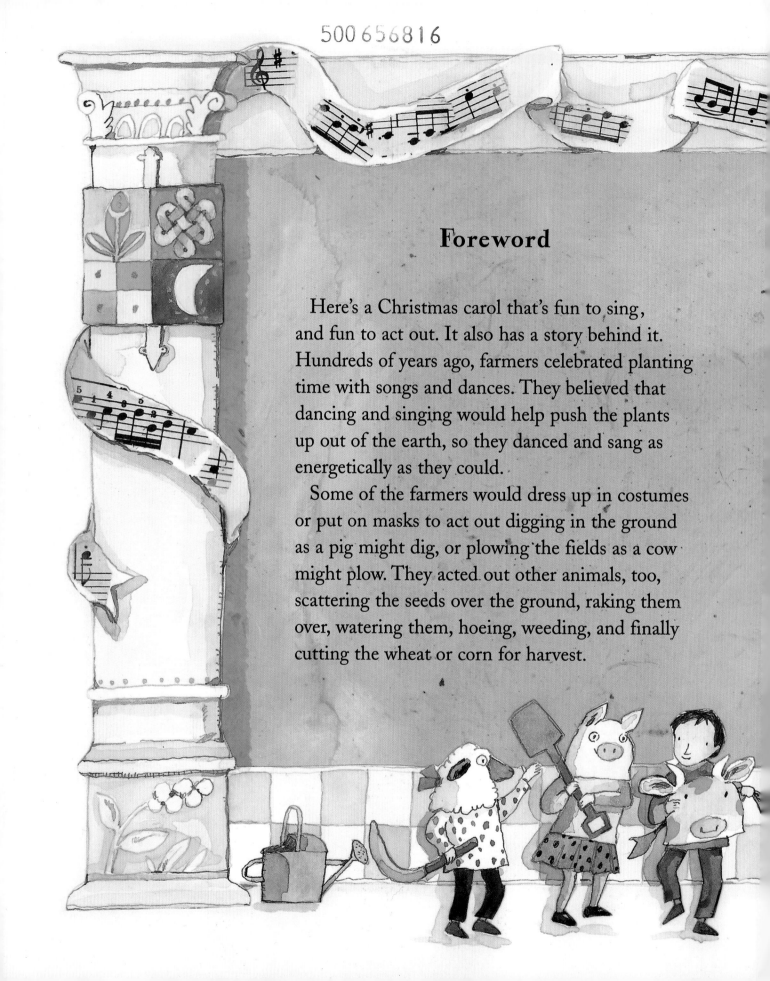

Foreword

Here's a Christmas carol that's fun to sing, and fun to act out. It also has a story behind it. Hundreds of years ago, farmers celebrated planting time with songs and dances. They believed that dancing and singing would help push the plants up out of the earth, so they danced and sang as energetically as they could.

Some of the farmers would dress up in costumes or put on masks to act out digging in the ground as a pig might dig, or plowing the fields as a cow might plow. They acted out other animals, too, scattering the seeds over the ground, raking them over, watering them, hoeing, weeding, and finally cutting the wheat or corn for harvest.

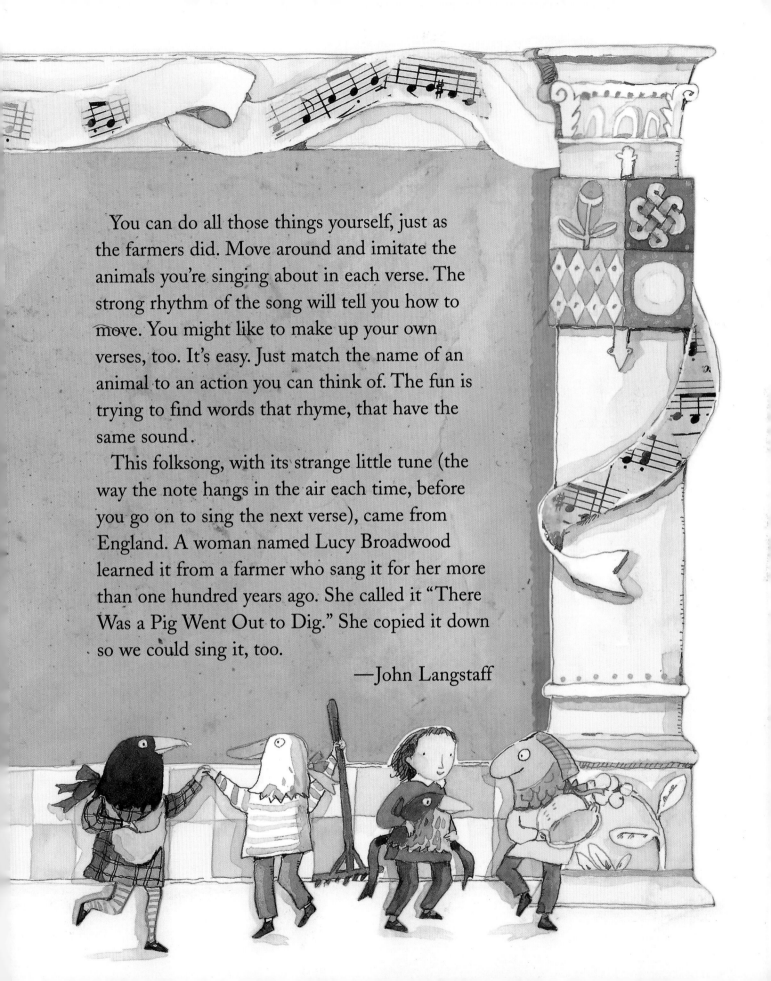

You can do all those things yourself, just as the farmers did. Move around and imitate the animals you're singing about in each verse. The strong rhythm of the song will tell you how to move. You might like to make up your own verses, too. It's easy. Just match the name of an animal to an action you can think of. The fun is trying to find words that rhyme, that have the same sound.

This folksong, with its strange little tune (the way the note hangs in the air each time, before you go on to sing the next verse), came from England. A woman named Lucy Broadwood learned it from a farmer who sang it for her more than one hundred years ago. She called it "There Was a Pig Went Out to Dig." She copied it down so we could sing it, too.

—John Langstaff

There was a pig
went out to dig,
On Christmas Day,
On Christmas Day.
There was a pig
Went out to dig
On Christmas Day
In the morning!

There was a cow
Went out to plow,
On Christmas Day,
On Christmas Day.
There was a cow
Went out to plow
On Christmas Day
In the morning!

There was a sparrow
Went out to harrow,
On Christmas Day,
On Christmas Day.
There was a sparrow
Went out to harrow
On Christmas Day
In the morning!

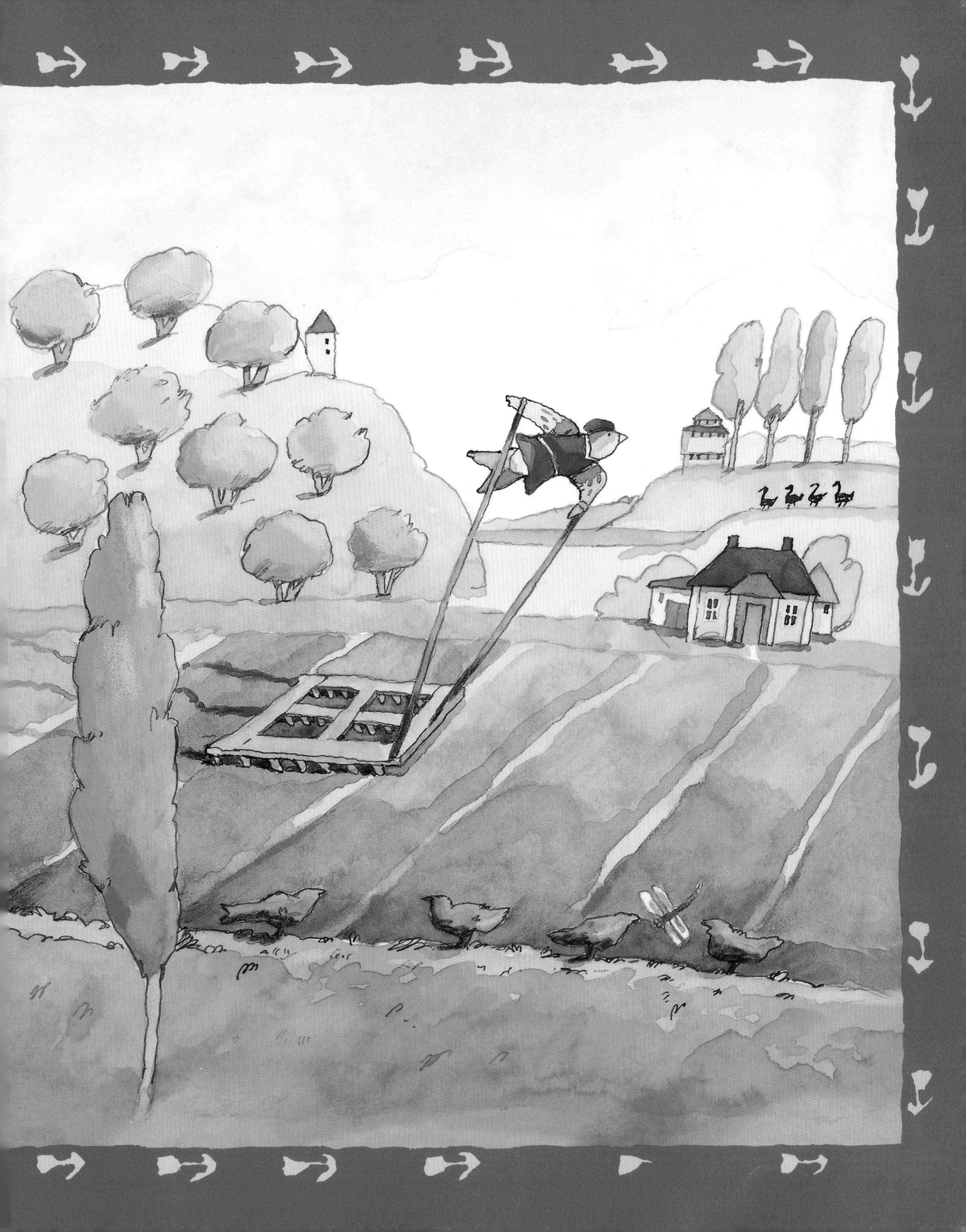

There was a crow
went out to sow,
On Christmas Day,
On Christmas Day.
There was a crow
Went out to sow
On Christmas Day
In the morning!

There was a sheep
went out to reap,
On Christmas Day,
On Christmas Day.
There was a sheep
Went out to reap
On Christmas Day
In the morning!

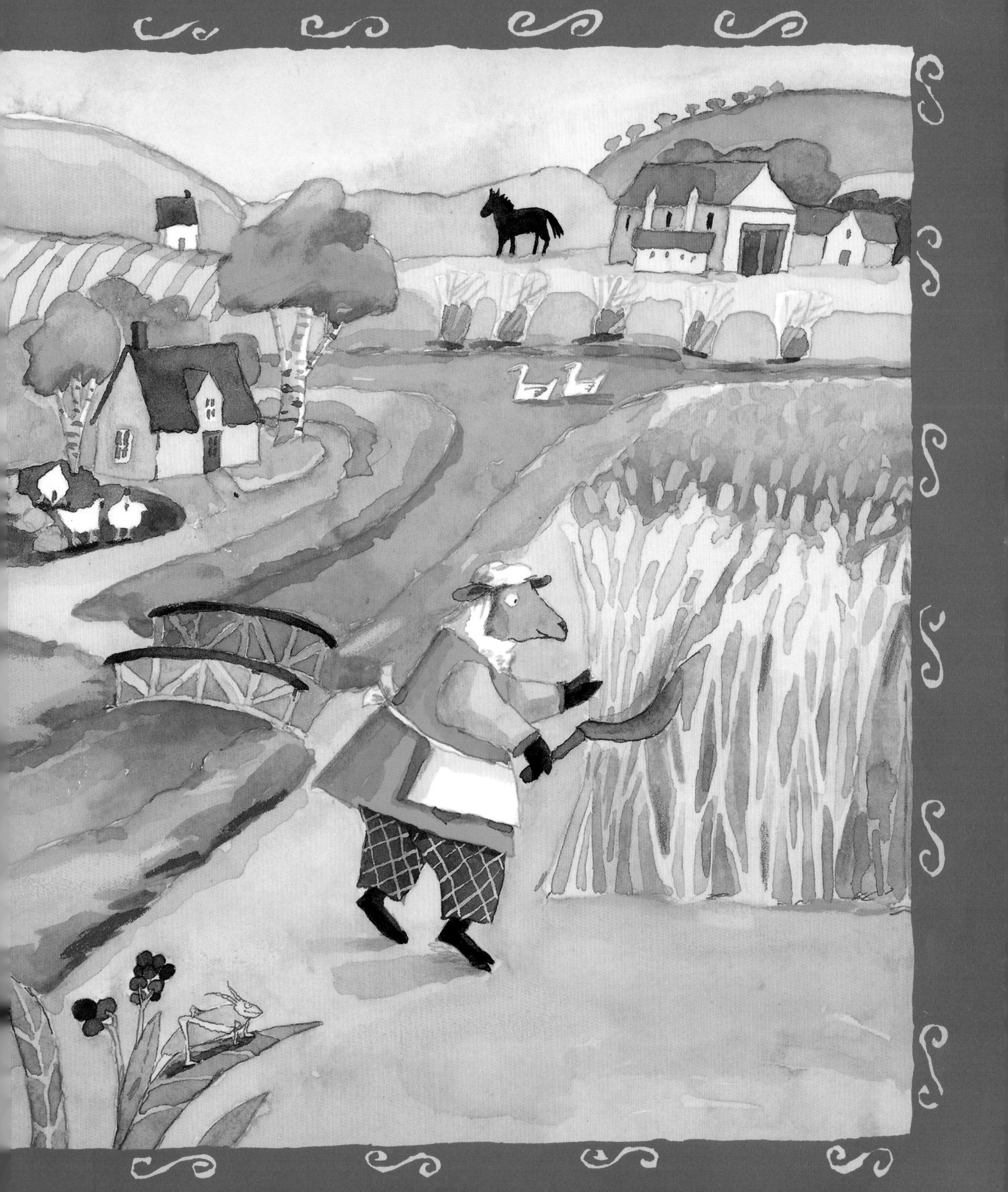

There was a drake
went out to rake,
On Christmas Day,
On Christmas Day.
There was a drake
Went out to rake
On Christmas Day
In the morning!

There was a minnow
Went out to winnow,
On Christmas Day,
On Christmas Day.
There was a minnow
Went out to winnow
On Christmas Day
In the morning!

Then every beast prepared the feast,
On Christmas Day, on Christmas Day.

**Then every beast prepared the feast
On Christmas Day in the morning!**

Let every creature on Earth now sing,
On Christmas Day,
On Christmas Day.
Let every creature on Earth now sing
On Christmas Day in the morning!

Christmas Day

There was a pig went out to dig, Chris - i - mas Day,

Chris - i - mas Day. There was a pig went out to dig On

Chris - i - mas Day in the morn - ing!

There was a cow went out to plow . . .

There was a sparrow went out to harrow . . .

There was a crow went out to sow . . .

There was a sheep went out to reap . . .

There was a drake went out to rake . . .

There was a minnow went out to winnow . . .

·~ Illustrator Notes ·~:

In preparation for illustrating *On Christmas Day in the Morning*, I researched the many symbols and images associated with the Christmas season. These rich symbols, connected to nature, agriculture, and the cycle of seasons, had their beginnings long before the birth of Jesus Christ, and continue to remind us of joy, abundance, and rebirth.

Mistletoe Mistletoe was sacred to the Norse goddess of love and marriage, Frigga. It is neither tree nor shrub, but a plant that grows and seeds itself in the branches of trees, never touching the ground. It was considered good luck to be kissed beneath mistletoe, so people hung mistletoe high in doorways and in stables.

Oak To the Celtic and Norse people, the oak tree was a sacred symbol that represented regeneration, rebirth, and endurance. During the winter solstice, when the branches were bare, Celts decorated oak trees with gilded apples and candles.

Holly The Romans believed that the leaves of holly remained green and the berries red throughout the year so that the world would still be beautiful even after other trees had dropped their leaves.

Laurel The ancient Romans used laurel (or bay leaf) during the winter Saturnalia celebration as a symbol of triumph and eternity because when the plant dies, its foliage does not wilt. The Romans made wreaths of laurel and hung them from their doorways during winter, a practice that carried on after the spread of Christianity.

Christmas Rose The Christmas Rose is an actual rose native to the mountains of central Europe, where it blooms in winter. Three Christmas Roses together symbolize light, love, and life.

Pomegranate In ancient Greece, the pomegranate fruit was associated with Persephone, the goddess who brought the spring each year. Because the pomegranate is full of seeds, it symbolized fertility and represented a return of life, as well as boundless love.

Wheat I've used a sheaf of wheat as a reminder of the yearly work of growing and harvesting carried out by laborers in the fields. It was and continues to be an apt symbol for Earth's bounty and life's abundance.

Crow's
farm

Cow's
farm

Sparrow's
farm

Drake's
farm

Pig's
farm

Sheep's
farm

Minnow's
farm

MELISSA SWEET has illustrated more than forty children's books, including the popular Pinky and Rex books by James Howe, and *Love and Kisses* by Sarah Wilson. She lives and works in Portland, Maine.

JOHN LANGSTAFF has spent much of his life sharing his love of music with audiences young and old. He was the national artistic director of Revels, Inc. Mr. Langstaff was born on Christmas Eve in Brooklyn Heights, New York. He lives in Massachusetts.